TONY HAWK'S
900 revolution

VOLUME 9

Tony Hawk's 900 Revolution
is published by Stone Arch Books
a Capstone imprint, 1710 Roe Crest Drive, North Mankato, MN
56003 www.capstonepub.com Copyright © 2013 by Stone
Arch Books All rights reserved. No part of this publication
may be reproduced in whole or in part, or stored in a retrieval
system, or transmitted in any form or by any means,
electronic, mechanical, photocopying, recording, or otherwise,
without written permission of the publisher.

Cataloging-in-Publication Data is available on the Library
of Congress website.
ISBN: 978-1-4342-3840-5 (library binding)
ISBN: 978-1-4342-4898-5 (paperback)

Summary: Once more beset by visions, Omar finds himself
trapped inside one. The world he sees is vastly different than
the one he left. In this postapocalyptic vision, the Collective
has defeated the Revolution. In their absence, the disbanded
Revolution has been replaced by a group of tribes that skate
in their honor. Omar searches for his friends, for the meaning
behind this horrific vision, and for a way out!

Photo and Vector Graphics Credits: Shutterstock.
Photo credit page 122, Bart Jones/Tony Hawk

Cover Illustrator: Wilson Toltosa
Cover Colorist: Benny Fuentes
Graphic Designer: Kay Fraser

Printed in China.
092012
006936RRDS13

ZOMBIFIED

BY BLAKE A. HOENA // ILLUSTRATED BY CAIO MAJADO

VOLUME 9

STONE ARCH BOOKS
a capstone imprint

TONY HAWK LANDED THE FIRST-EVER 900.

1

Omar slowly blinked his eyes open. He wasn't ready to get out of bed and start a brand new day. As he stared up at the ceiling of his bedroom, the edges of his vision were fuzzy. He wanted to think it was because none of this was real. That what had happened over the past few days was all a bad dream.

That he would be able to crawl out of bed, throw on his Birdhouse T-shirt and a worn pair of Vans, and hit the ramps in their training facility, as if he hadn't a care in the world.

That Joey, Dylan, and Amy would already be waiting at the breakfast table for him. Joey would tell a bad joke every time Dylan took a sip of OJ to try to get his buddy to snort juice out his nose as he laughed.

Amy would berate them for being a couple of immature boys, yet she'd think their antics were just as funny as they did.

That Eldrick, their mentor, would coolly walk in and throw them a disapproving glance as he sat down to eat breakfast with them.

That Neelu, Eldrick's daughter, would secretly wink at him with her sparkling brown eyes whenever her father wasn't looking.

These were all things Omar had secretly enjoyed since joining the Revolution. And what teenager wouldn't love being part of an action sports team that not only consisted of some of the world's best athletes in their sport, but also had a secret mission...

Save the world!

That was, until yesterday, when everything changed. Their secret complex had been infiltrated by the bad guys, the Collective. They had stolen what Omar and his friends in the Revolution had fought so hard to gather: the Fragments of the skateboard that Tony Hawk used to complete the first-ever 900.

The quest still seemed odd to Omar, even though he was living it. But owning a piece of that board—one of its composite wheels—Omar was aware of its power.

The skateboard could unlock powers in anyone who came into possession of one of its pieces.

Now, Omar was afraid that as soon as he stepped outside his bedroom, reality would hit him like a Mack truck. That Eldrick would be mad. No, beyond mad. More like incensed at what had happened and blame them. His friends would be angry and screaming at each other. Their quest would be lost beyond hope, and the Revolution would fall apart.

Omar sat up in bed and groaned in pain. His legs were stiff. Arms rubbery. A coping-shaped welt ran across his back. After the theft was discovered, he hit the training room's halfpipe and skated angrily, pushing himself to his limits and beyond.

Omar thought that maybe if he could perform a 900 himself, everything would be better. All the disappointment and anger of the past few days would disappear. But even with a Fragment, he couldn't achieve what Tony Hawk had done those many years ago during the X Games.

Now his forearms were covered in raspberries. His right knee clicked funny as he stretched it out. Omar had been too mad to even bother putting on pads, and he was paying for it.

Omar kicked off his blankets and rolled out of bed. He grabbed a T-shirt off the floor and slipped it over his head. He picked up a pair of khakis tossed over a chair and slid them on. The teen was a wrinkled, stinky mess, but he didn't care.

It was over.

The Revolution.

Time to face the music.

***

Omar Grebes pushed his door open and listened to see if anyone else was awake in the complex. After the theft, and knowing that the Collective now knew where they were, he'd be surprised if anyone had gotten a good night's sleep. The hallway outside his room was still dark, and everything was quiet. Too quiet.

"Ames?" he called.

"Slider?"

"Joey?"

"Neelu?"

And lastly, "Eldrick?"

Nothing.

The only response was the echo of his voice bouncing endlessly down the complex's long hallway, quieter and quieter.

Omar strolled into the kitchen and turned on the light switch.

Nothing.

He flicked the switch up and down a few times with no results. "Aw, come on," he groaned.

In the dark, he fumbled around the kitchen, snatched a bowl and spoon from the cupboard, grabbed a half-empty box of Wheaty O's from the pantry, and pulled out a half-gallon of vanilla soy milk from the fridge. As he sat down, Omar noticed that the kitchen table was covered in a layer of dust.

Hope it's not my week for kitchen duty, he thought.

Omar filled his bowl to overflowing with cereal and then poured the soy milk. He gagged as it slid out of the carton in thick, oozing chunks.

I'm gonna hurl, he thought as he ran to the kitchen sink. *Guess I'm not getting breakfast here.*

As he walked back down the hallway, wiping spittle off his chin, he poked his head into Joey's room, and then Slider's, and lastly Amy's. They were all gone.

Probably in search of some grub, too, he thought.

Back in his room, Omar pulled his skateboard out from under his bed. The decals on the deck were nearly rubbed off from hard riding.

He looked at the right front wheel and casually flicked it with his index figure. As it spun, blue electricity emitted from the wheel. This was his Fragment. His piece of Tony Hawk's 900 board. His talisman.

Omar then grabbed a backpack and quickly sifted through its contents: a few power bars, a half-full water bottle, a hoodie, an MP3 player, and some earbuds.

"Ah, just what I need," he said aloud. "Some tunes."

Omar flicked the MP3 to his "death rattle" playlist. It was filled with hardcore bands, like Spyd3r SpAnk and Brown Haze, and was perfect for letting off some steam, which he really needed to do right now.

Omar kicked his board down the hall and leaped on. Music throbbing in his ears, he exited the Revolution's now-not-so-secret complex, and skated into a bright new day.

2

Omar skated out of a sewer culvert and into one of Phoenix's suburbs. This was his favorite exit from the complex. There was an iHop only a few blocks away. The morning waitress was pretty cute. He had been flirting with her for the past couple of months and had been laying the groundwork for asking her out.

Omar figured Neelu was playing too hard to get, not to mention her dad was always hovering over them when they tried to talk, so thought it smarter to find someone a little more accessible. And it'd be nice to have someone to hang out with and talk about non-Revolution stuff. Someone who smelled good—not like dirt and sweat—after a rough mission.

So Omar headed in the iHop's direction.

It must be pretty early in the AM, he thought. The sun hovered low in the sky, and a dark red haze stretched out along the horizon. Plus, the streets were empty: not a car, biker, or skater to be seen. The stillness only confused him about Joey, Amy, and Slider's absence. They weren't early birds, unless they couldn't sleep either after the complex had been robbed, and they had all decided to head over to iHop for some grub, too. It served 24/7. But why wouldn't they ask him to tag along? He just hoped Neelu wasn't there. Then he'd never have the courage to ask for the waitress's number.

Since there wasn't any traffic, Omar wove his way down the middle of the street. Every now and then, as he skated, he'd do a nose stall or grind on a curb and then keep on going. He didn't want to do anything too tricky this morning as he was still feeling the effects of his skate session yesterday.

"Aw, come on!" he shouted as he approached the iHop. The place was dark. Closed.

His stomach grumbled.

I'm gonna starve, he thought.

Omar looked around. The houses along the street seemed oddly quiet. No lights were on.

No alarms clocks buzzing. No radios spitting out early morning talk-show banter. No one stepping out to get the morning newspaper off their front stoop. Heck, there weren't any papers to get.

This was past being a ghost town.

It was scary dead.

Then he noticed them. A group of kids, all slightly younger than Omar, on BMX bikes. They wore ripped jeans and tattered T-shirts and baseball caps representing various teams. Something about them gave Omar the creeps. He skated into the street and continued on his way, not daring to glance back at the bikers to see if they were following him.

He actually didn't need to. His Fragment was aware of his tension and began to crackle with life. As it popped and fizzled, Omar's senses came alive. He could feel every dimple in the pavement under his composite wheels, hear the gears of four BMX bikes clicking into chain links, and smell the BO of the BMXers he had seen. They were not far behind.

Omar decided to pick it up a notch. He pushed his board harder to build up speed. He didn't need to look back to know the BMXers had done the same.

Omar knew it'd be hard to outdistance them.

It'd be hard for any skater to outrace a BMXer, even with a Fragment. So Omar was looking for terrain that would give him an advantage, like a stair railing to grind down or a retaining walls to ollie over, but the Phoenix area was so flat that all Omar could do was skate down the middle of the street. He might as well have had a bull's-eye plastered to his back.

At one point, he saw the BMXers catching up to him on his right, so he cut left down a side street. A little while later, they were on his left, so he swerved right. It wasn't until he saw that some of the side streets were blocked by other BMXers carrying bats and hockey sticks that he realized he was being herded somewhere.

Did a gang of BMXers take over this part of town? Omar wondered.

He did a 180 and road goofy so he could look back and take in his pursuers. They didn't have the look or feel of the Collective. They were too disorganized to be part of an evil plot to take over the world. Maybe they could be some other group. Whoever they were, Omar didn't take kindly to this treatment.

On the next side street, Omar turned to face the BMXer blocking his path and skated directly at her. She held her bat out menacingly.

As she waved it at him, Omar kicked into an ollie as high as he could, flying over her bat, her handlebars, and clipping her shoulder. She gaped at him in awe as he sailed over her and then landed on the street beyond.

Now these newbs are going to see some skating, Omar thought.

And the chase was on.

Omar pushed his board forward. Blue electricity sparked from its wheels. Behind him, he could hear the BMXers shout to one another. They were angered by him ruining their plans. A few blocks later, he could hear their labored breaths as the chase wore on.

The landscape opened up into a large parking lot for a school. Empty buses and cars littered the pavement. Now he could lose these bozos.

About six BMXers were in pursuit. He let the nearest one catch up to him as he headed toward the side of a car. As he neared it, Omar leaped high into the air, clearing the roof of the car as his board continued to roll under it. It was a trick he learned from watching videos of Flyin' Brian Beardsley. After flying over the roof of the car, he landed on his board and kept going. There was a satisfying crunch behind him as the BMXer crashed into the side of the car.

Just a few meters ahead was a bus. Two of the BMXers, waving hockey sticks, converged on Omar—one from the right and one from the left. They were whooping loudly, ready to strike a deathblow. Omar quickly ducked down on his board, hands on the pavement, and mimicked some Jay Adam's street-style skating to wheel his way under the bus.

The BMXers cursed at him as they slid to a halt beside the bus.

Omar popped up on his board on the other side and brushed off his hands. They were scraped and raw after that trick, but his pursuers had quickly been cut down to three.

Omar looped in and around the parked vehicles. The course slowed the BMXers down just enough that Omar could stay ahead of them. But he was growing tired of this game. He needed a way out.

Omar saw it up ahead. A fence, two meters high, wrapped around one corner of the parking lot. Omar headed for it. He could sense the BMXers close behind. Their hot breath. The sweat dripping down their backs. They didn't know what he was going to do—probably thought they had their prey trapped as they couldn't imagine anyone could conceive such a trick.

But they didn't have a Fragment. Didn't know what it could do.

Omar kicked his board into an ollie. He flew through the air. Reaching down with one hand to hold his deck, he stretched out for the top of the fence with his other hand. As he grabbed it, he used his momentum to swing his legs over the fence while still holding his board between his feet.

The landing hurt. Felt like he kicked a brick wall. Like his knee joints were butting rams. But he landed the trick and then slowly rolled away as the BMXers skidded into the fence.

Their choice was either climb the fence or ride around it. In either case, Omar would be long gone before they made it to the other side. Their curses bounced off his back.

CLAP! CLAP! CLAP! Omar was startled by the sound of applause off to his side.

"Haven't seen someone land a trick like that since back in the day of the Revolution," a voice shouted.

A familiar voice. With a familiar ring of sarcasm.

Omar turned to see who had yelled at him and was stunned.

"Joey?"

3

"Joey?" Omar couldn't believe his eyes. His friend was sitting on a BMX bike on his side of the fence.

"Funny seeing you here, O," Joey said. "After disappearing like that, I mean."

"What? Me?" Omar wasn't sure what Joey was talking about.

"Yeah, right after the break in," Joey said.

He kicked his board over to his friend. Joey got off his bike, and the two of them stood eye to eye, or more like eye to chin since Joey seemed taller and more muscular than Omar remembered. As if his friend had aged several years overnight. His peach fuzz had grown into a scruffy beard.

Joey's blond hair was unkempt and long. Even his clothes appeared aged and worn, as if he hadn't changed them in days. Or weeks.

"It's been years, O," Joey said.

"Years?" Omar asked.

"Yeah, we thought you'd gone into hiding," Joey continued. "Afraid to show yourself after the mess the Collective made of things."

"I have no idea what you're talking about," Omar said. "The break-in happened just yesterday."

"O, it happened almost five years ago," Joey replied.

Omar looked over his friend more closely. That's the only thing that could explain the changes he saw in Joey. How his once easy-going smile had transformed into more of a sneer. How the glint of youth in his eyes had been dulled, probably by seeing things he shouldn't have. That no one should have.

Joey motioned around him. To the silent world. The empty houses. The stranded cars.

"This is the world that the Collective wrought," he said. "This is the result of that fateful day."

Heck, Omar thought, *even his words seem older, more mature. Deeper.*

Then Joey's tired eyes bore down on Omar.

"This is your fault, for abandoning us when we needed you most." Joey poked Omar in the chest with an accusatory finger. "You did this."

"Me?" Omar sounded defeated.

It felt like a dream. Surreal. Like that movie *28 Days Later*, where a dude wakes up in a hospital twenty-eight days after slipping into a coma, and the world has changed. Is full of evil.

"Joey, look at me," Omar pleaded. "Do I look like I'm five years older than when you saw me last?"

Joey's eyes narrowed. It was uncanny, to Omar, seeing his friend with such intense eyes, as if they were boring through him.

"No, you don't," Joey admitted. And for a second, there was a playful glimmer in Joey's eyes. "Heck of a beauty sleep."

And then Joey did something totally unexpected. He stepped up to Omar and wrapped his arms around his friend in a bear hug.

"I missed you, O," Joey's voice cracked.

"Ugh!" Omar gasped in Joey's grip. "I missed you, too, but your smotherin' me."

Joey unwrapped his arms and placed his hands on Omar's shoulders.

The intensity of his eyes was back as he looked at Omar. "Things are gonna change now. Now that you're back," Joey said.

Then he looked around them. A circle of BMXers had gathered. They stood looking on nervously.

"Sorry if my crew gave you a scare," Joey said.

"No, nothing I couldn't handle," Omar winked.

"We just need to be wary of strangers, is all," Joey explained. "Now we've been out in the open a little too long. Let's head back to base."

Like a well-oiled team, the BMXers all hopped on their bikes and headed out. Joey got on his and turned back to Omar.

"You'd better come with us," Joey commanded. "So let's do a little tailgating like old times."

Omar grabbed the back of Joey's bike, and they were off.

Their pace was quick and steady. Omar was led away from the school and back down the road the BMXers had originally chased him. Eventually, the road led to a large supermarket. Around the supermarket stood a wall, a circle of cars and trucks, and on top of the vehicles all sorts of garbage was piled: grocery carts, garbage cans, bookshelves, and wooden crates.

Joey stopped about a block from the store's parking lot. The BMXers seemed nervous as they shifted their weight from one foot to another.

"You think you can keep up with us?" Joey said, turning to Omar.

"I've held my own so far," Omar joked.

"What happens next ain't no game," Joey said. And there it was again, the hardness in his eyes. "What happens next is life or death. But all we need to do is make it to the other side of that wall of cars."

"Simple enough," Omar said, knowing there was something bad that Joey wasn't telling him.

"Stay close to me, O," Joey said. "Now head out!"

The other BMXers fanned out, pulling out various weapons: baseball bats, hockey sticks, and broomsticks. They headed toward the supermarket.

As they passed a row of houses near the store, chaos broke out. The doors of the houses flew open and people streamed out of them. More people jumped through windows, burst from garage doors, and sprouted from manhole covers. Some rode bikes. Others rode skateboards. But most of them just ran wildly with flailing arms.

The sight of these people freaked Omar out.

What frightened him most was their screaming. It was almost inhuman.

"Keep up," Joey shouted back at him.

Omar dug in, kicking his board forward. Sparks flew from the wheels of his skateboard as he picked up speed.

They were racing forward, and the screaming people where converging on Joey's crew. The ones on bikes and skateboards were getting closer. Omar was afraid he wouldn't make it to the wall fast enough. And once they did, how would he get over it.

On both sides of him, Omar saw BMXers swinging away with their weapons. They were knocking people off their boards. Tipping over bikes. Blood splattered everywhere, but it didn't stop the mad rush of people converging on them.

As they approached the wall, Omar was amazed to see the back doors of several delivery truck trailers fall open. The BMXers quickly road up the doors like ramps, and then the doors slammed shut behind them.

A door opened in front of Joey and Omar. Joey rode up the ramp. Omar was close behind. And so were a handful of screaming maniacs. They seemed to be running faster than he thought normal people could.

TONY HAWK'S 900 REVOLUTION

Omar tried to speed up as he felt hands reaching for him. He was up the ramp and skating through the truck's back, which served as a tunnel through the wall of vehicles and garbage.

The truck's door was pulled shut behind them, but not before one of the people also made it through.

On the other side, Omar skated down a ramp, and then stalled his board. He turned just as the person leaped from the truck. He felt hands, wiry as steel cables, wrap around his throat, and then he fell backwards. All the while the person was screaming and spitting in his face.

As Omar struggled against the weight that held him down, he looked into the person's eyes. What frightened him more than the crazed screaming was the fact that the person's eyes were red. Blood red. He also had unnaturally reddish hair and a pinkish hue to his skin.

Joey grabbed a hockey stick from one of the BMXers and casually walked up to the struggling pair.

THUNK!

Joey whacked the person across the back of his skull. He fell motionless, a dead weight bearing down on Omar.

"Toss him over the wall," Joey commanded.

- 29 -

"Are you just going to let him go?" one of his crew asked.

"It's either that or kill him," Joey said in a tone so menacing that Omar could not believe the words had come from his friend's mouth.

A couple of the BMXers quickly moved to obey his original command.

"Welcome to Clan Rail HQ," Joey joked.

"Your headquarters is a supermarket?" Omar asked.

They were sitting on milk crates in front of a small fire, which was just outside the double doors of a large grocery store.

"Yeah, pretty lame, I know," Joey replied as he and Omar started eating a meal of canned peas. "But it's better than the mall. Food's pretty scarce, and here, we have a year's supply of these."

Joey held up the nearly empty can of peas and smirked. "Man, I hate peas."

"So who were those people that attacked us?" Omar asked.

"Zombies."

"As in the undead?" asked Omar.

"Might as well be," Joey replied. "But nah, that's just what we call them."

"They don't eat brains, do they?"asked Omar.

Joey laughed. "No, not that type of zombie. They're just what's left of humanity after the Collective got its way. Husks of flesh. Soulless."

"But what about you," said Omar. "You're still fighting them, aren't you? The Collective hasn't won."

Joey tipped his can upside down and let the last of the peas roll into his mouth. He chewed slowly, as if contemplating Omar's question. "We're twenty riders strong, O," he said. "No match for what's out there. No match for the Collective. We're just fighting to survive. That's all."

"What about your Fragment?" asked Omar.

"The Collective has all the Fragments but one," Joey replied. "That wheel of yours. No amount of searching could locate it, which is why I thought you went into hiding. And your Fragment is the only thing preventing the complete end of humanity as we know it."

"What about the others?" asked Omar. "Eldrick?"

"Dead."

Omar's heart sank.

Omar almost didn't dare to ask, "And Rafe?"

"Dead," said Joey.

"Neelu?" Omar's voice quavered a bit.

"O, I don't even want to tell you. It might be easier to tell you who's not dead, like Amy."

"Really?" Omar sounded hopeful.

"Yeah, she's head of Clan Kestrel," Joey added.

"And Slider?"

"I think we'd better stop there." Joey's voice grew quiet and his eyes glistened in the firelight.

"Why? Was he the traitor? Is that why the Collective was able to break into our complex?" Omar asked, a hint of anger and suspicion tinting the tone of his voice.

A look of pure rage flashed across Joey's eyes and then was gone so quickly that Omar questioned whether he actually saw Joey's sudden change of emotion.

"No," said Joey. "And if you ever bring up Slider's name and the word 'traitor' in the same breath again, our friendship ends. Right then and there."

Joey stood up and turned to walk away. But Omar leaped to his feet, chasing after his friend and grabbing Joey's shoulder.

"Sorry, man," said Omar. "But I just want to know what happened to our friends."

"I'll leave Slider's story for Amy to tell." Joey's voice was quiet.

The way he said "Slider's story" made Omar believe that it wasn't a fairy tale with a happily-ever-after ending. That it was a tragic tale. A Romeo-and-Juliet-type story.

"Can we go see Amy?" Omar asked.

"Sure, I figured you'd want to," Joey said. "It'll be a long ride across the desert. We'll leave at dusk to avoid the heat. So better get some shuteye now. It's a dangerous ride, and I need you to have your wits about you."

"Freedy," Joey shouted. "Show Omar to a bunk."

One of Joey's crew jumped out of the shadows to do as Joey had asked. He was a short youth, probably only twelve years old. He led Omar inside the supermarket and to a storage room. As soon as they were out of sight of everyone else, Freedy turned his attention to Omar's board.

"Is it true?" Freedy asked. "Is that the missing Fragment?" Freedy pointed to the right rear wheel of Omar's board.

"Yeah, I guess so," Omar replied.

"Never thought I'd see it," Freedy said. "It's pretty valuable, you know. The Collective has offered a year's supply of food for just a rumor of it. Ya know, like cheeseburgers and fries smothered in ketchup. We haven't had..."

Something in the excitement of Freedy's voice disturbed Omar. He was salivating at the mere thought of food and getting a far-off look, as if he'd do anything for something to nosh on other than canned peas. As Joey had said, this is the world the Collective wrought. A hungry world where people barely survived.

As a precaution, once Freedy showed him his bunk, which was some storage racks with a few blankets for padding, Omar pulled the Fragment off its truck. The wheel sizzled with blue energy as he did. He tucked it into his front pants pocket. Nobody was going to take it from him without a fight.

5

Omar woke to far-off shouts. He wasn't sure what was happening, but he thought that he had heard Joey barking commands against a background of zombie screams.

Omar tossed aside his blanket and sat up in bed. He heard shuffling feet, and saw three dark shadows clinging to the walls.

"He's awake," one of them yelled.

"I've got his board," another shouted.

"Let's get going," the third called to his friends.

The three shadows stumbled over each other as they ran from the room. Omar listened to the echoes of their footsteps receding, but he didn't give chase. They had his board. That was replaceable.

In his front pocket, Omar still had the Fragment, and that wasn't replaceable.

Omar poked his head out of the storage closet. In front of the door lay Freedy. He was out cold with a nasty looking lump sprouting from his forehead.

"Freedy, wake up," Omar shook the youth.

Slowly, Freedy blinked his eyes awake. When he saw Omar, he looked worried.

"I tried to stop them," Freedy said. "I really did."

In the distance, Omar heard Joey's voice booming commands followed by a loud cacophony of noises. It sounded as if he was getting closer to the storage locker. So were the screams of the zombies.

"No worries, Freedy," Omar said, shooting the younger boy a smile. "They didn't get what they were after." Omar patted his front pocket. "It's still with me."

Freedy smiled weakly at the news.

"Say, where are the bikes?" Omar asked. "I think we're going to need them."

"A few are parked by the back door."

"I have a feeling that that's where Joey's going to be headed," said Omar. "Sounds like HQ is being overrun, and we need to get out of here."

Freedy's eyes widened in fear. "Really?"

"Yeah, so lead the way, and quick!"

Freedy leaped to his feet. They wove their way through aisles of half-empty shelves, heading for the back door.

Omar was right. Joey was headed in that direction, too. And from the sounds of it, he was being followed by a howling mass of zombies.

Omar and Freedy reached the bikes moments before Joey. There were nine of them. Freedy pointed out that there were also emergency packs stashed with the bikes. Omar noticed 12 packs, so the three thieves must have headed out this way, too. Hopefully that was a good sign that their escape route was clear.

Joey burst in on them with nine of his crew.

"I thought you two would be here, and..." Joey's voice trailed as he spotted the remaining bikes and did the math in his head. Nine bikes and twelve of them.

Omar was one step ahead of him. He pulled his Fragment out of his pocket. "I don't need a bike."

He focused on the Fragment, and it began to emit blue sparks. Then suddenly, in his hand was a skateboard very similar to the one that had just been stolen from him. Only this one sparked with blue energy from nose to tail.

"That takes care of you," Joey said with a commanding voice. He sounded so confident that Omar wasn't sure it came from his friend's mouth. He was still getting used to this new, older Joey.

"Freedy, you're with me," Joey said. Then turning to two other members of the Rail Clan, he added, "Nick and Kat, you pair up."

Omar threw his board on the ground and hopped on, pushing himself forward through the back door. As he exited the supermarket, he snagged a pack and slung it over his shoulder in one fluid motion.

Joey and the other BMXers were right behind him. Omar paused for a second, to wait for Joey to take the lead. As he did, he saw the room behind them filling up with mad, writhing bodies.

One of the BMXers slammed the back door shut while another jammed a bolt in place to keep it closed.

BANG! BANG! BANG!

"That won't hold them for long," Joey shouted. "So let's get out of here."

It was easy to see the direction that the thieves had taken. The front and back doors of the trailer were open. Joey, Omar, and crew rode up the ramp, through the trailer, and down the ramp on the other side.

Finally, they were beyond the wall. No zombies to be seen. They must have broken in another way.

A couple blocks ahead of them, they could see the backs of the thieves riding away.

A menacing smirk crossed Joey's face. "They seem to be escaping in the direction we want to go," he said.

Omar didn't know if that was really true or not, but he followed Joey as he sped off.

6

Screaming erupted around them.

As Joey, Omar, and the members of Clan Rail
sped through the supermarket's parking lot, a wall of
zombies suddenly came at them from both sides. They
were running, biking, skateboarding, and some were
even on scooters. The scene would have been almost
comical if not for the crazed look in their blood-red
eyes. Or, of course, the flesh falling from their bodies.

Joey took the lead, not waiting for his crew. He
seemed to trust that they'd make it beyond the wall of
zombies that was about to crush them like a giant trash
compactor. Joey's sights were on the three thieves up
ahead.

Omar kept pace with him, amazed that his constructed skateboard glided effortlessly across the parking lot. It was as if there wasn't any friction between wheels and pavement. It was the smoothest ride ever, and his speed was only limited by how hard he pushed himself forward.

Even with Freedy riding double with him, it didn't take long for Joey to catch up to the three thieves. Freedy stuck a hockey stick in the front spokes of one of the rider's bikes, and the rider flipped over his handlebars, landing hard on the pavement. One of the remaining pair looked back to see what had happened, and that moment of hesitation was all Omar needed to glide up beside him and pull him from his bike.

The third rider skidded to a halt and spun his bike around to face Joey. He must have known that fleeing was useless.

"It's not what you're thinking," the kid said.

"You don't know what I'm thinking," Joey scowled. He got off his bike and strode over to the kid. Before the kid could reply, Joey shoved him hard. The kid fell backwards, off his bike.

On his back, the kid had a pack. He reached inside it and pulled out Omar's skateboard.

"Here," he said. "We didn't want to take it. We had to. You know, for food."

Joey grabbed the board and showed it to Omar. "Do you want this?" he asked.

"Nah, this board's doing the trick," Omar said, resting one foot on his new deck.

The three thieves looked at Omar's electric blue board and let out a collective sigh of defeat.

"Yeah, that's right," Joey said. "You didn't get want you were after. But now you're going to get what's coming to you."

Just then, the other BMXers joined them. A block away was the mass of zombies, still howling after their prey.

"You better get running," Joey told the three thieves.

"Running?"

"You don't mean?"

"What about our bikes?"

"Just so happens, I need three bikes." Joey laughed. "Omar, you really should use one of these. That board of yours is going to draw a lot of unwanted attention."

Omar picked up his board, and it quickly dissolved into an ordinary composite wheel, which he stuffed into his front pocket.

Then he hopped on one of the bikes.

"Freedy and Kat." Joey nodded toward the other two bikes. "Those are yours."

And then they were off.

Looking back, the three thieves were on foot, racing away from the mob of skating, biking, running, and howling zombies.

Omar turned to Joey. "Don't you feel bad, leaving them behind like that?"

"It's what they deserve," Joey said coldly.

Omar realized that Joey had changed during those missing years. The Joey he knew would never leave someone to suffer that sort of fate, not even an enemy. This new Joey was a meaner, less forgiving version of the Joey he had originally befriended.

"Besides," Joey added. "We have a few secret escape routes around here. If they make it to one of them, they'll be fine."

7

Omar was amazed at how suddenly the city ended. It appeared to sprawl out forever, especially under the exertion of pedaling in the hot sun. But then one minute he was listening to the dull hum of rubber on pavement; the next he was hearing the crunch of his knobby tires bite into sand.

This made the ride more difficult. Omar wasn't used to the way his muscles worked pumping pedals, and the rough sand threatened to throw him off balance with every rut.

Joey took the lead, and the rest of his crew lined up, single file, behind him. Omar started just in back of Joey.

Within an hour, he found himself second to last in the pack as riders got frustrated with his wobbly pace and passed him. Only Freedy was behind him.

At least someone else is struggling as much as me, Omar thought.

A couple hours later, Joey was so far ahead of Omar that he was almost out of sight, and the sun was dropping near the horizon. Joey crested a hill and called for a halt, waiting for everyone to catch up.

"Good thing I had Freedy keep on eye on you." Joey laughed as Omar stopped and nearly fell off his bike in exhaustion. "Otherwise, we may have lost you."

Omar looked back and saw Freedy spryly leap off his bike. There was hardly a bead of sweat on him while the pits and back of Omar's shirt were soaked.

Everyone busted out their packs, which were filled with bottles of water, cans of food and power bars, a flashlight, a Swiss army knife, a hoodie, and other survival gear. Joey had his crew ready for just about anything.

They all slugged down some water and noshed on power bars. Then the clan started putting on their hoodies. Omar was a little shocked, as it felt like a furnace out under the desert sun.

"You'd better follow suit," Joey nudged him. "The sun's almost down, and the temps will drop to near freezing before we reach our destination."

They also strapped flashlights to their handlebars, so Omar went to do the same. As he pulled out his flashlight, he noticed it was plugged into a wire that was embedded into the fabric of his pack.

"The packs have a solar skin," Freedy told him. "They act like chargers during the day, whether you plug in a flashlight, MP3 player, or camp stove."

Omar must have either look confused or amazed because Freedy added, "You ain't seen nothing yet. Wait until you see Clan Kestrel's HQ."

After some water and a bite to eat, Omar felt as if he could possibly keep pace with Joey's crew.

"Okay, let's head on out," Joey commanded. "And keep your eye out for creepers."

"Creepers?" Omar asked, turning to Freedy.

He just frowned.

With the sun setting and their surroundings turning black, Joey kept the dozen bikers close together. There was a heightened sense of awareness among the crew, and at every coyote yelp or owl hoot, someone would jerk their flashlight in the direction of the sound.

For the most part, all Omar heard was the crunch of his knobby tires digging into the packed sand of the trail. That's what he focused on, keeping his legs pumping and his bike moving forward. The night was a deep dark, and the stars were brilliant overhead. Now that the pace had slowed a bit and the temps were cooling, he was beginning to like this night riding.

A couple hours later, Joey called another halt. They quickly gulped down more water and chomped on some power bars. And then they were off within fifteen minutes. Hardly enough time for Omar to catch his breath. It helped, however, that his Fragment, glowing through his front pocket, was giving him a little boost, which allowed him to push through his exhaustion.

This part of the journey was across a long, flat stretch of desert. Omar could see the shadowy shapes of cacti and other desert plants flying by.

They were about to head up a dune when a loud screech broke the silence.

"Creepers!" someone yelled.

"Circle up," Joey commanded.

Again, Omar was impressed by how well Joey's crew reacted. They circled their bikes to form a protective perimeter with flashlights shining outward.

Then, to Omar's surprise, they all pulled their handlebars off their bikes, wielding them like clubs, and detached their front wheels, which they strapped to one arm like a shield. With Freedy's help, Omar followed.

What Omar saw next both shocked and frightened him. Creatures slowly crept out of the night. Creatures that looked like they were a jumble of animal parts— part reptile, part wolf, and part bird. Some crawled along the ground. Others fluttered just above the desert sand. Some had mouths filled with rows of fangs. Others had razor sharp beaks.

Before Omar could understand what was happening, the creatures rushed forward with growls and screeches.

Omar saw the BMXers next to him blocking attacks with their wheel shields and then striking expertly with their handlebar clubs. They amazed Omar. They made him wonder why he had ever been chosen to lead the Revolution, back when there still was a Revolution. Joey seemed to be doing a far better job with this rag-tag crew than he had ever done, even with the tutelage of Eldrick backing him up. Though, no matter how skilled they were, it didn't matter with the mass of creatures that were attacking them.

After what seemed like hours of blocking and striking, Omar saw the youth next to him slip and fall under the weight of a coyote-rattlesnake-owl creature. It raised its head, a mouth full of fangs dripping with venom, and was about to strike when Joey stepped into the fray and knocked the creature aside.

With one fallen member, they had to tighten their circle. Then someone else fell. Then another.

There seemed to be no end to the creatures, so they had no choice but to fight on.

That's when Omar saw it, the glow from his pocket. He noticed that the creatures seemed to be avoiding him and focusing their attack on the BMXers around him.

Omar dropped his club and dug his hand into his pocket. He pulled out his Fragment, which now was crackling excitedly with energy. He raised it over his head and, as if the Fragment had a mind of its own, it shot a brilliant bolt of blue light into the night sky.

The area around them lit up. And the Rail Clan would have despaired, seeing an completely endless sea of writhing animals parts, if it weren't for the fear reflecting off the creatures' eyes. Before the blue light had waned, they had all scattered, except for the dead and dying ones.

Joey quickly surveyed his crew. There were various injuries and a couple of the BMXers were a little wobbly on their feet, but no one was seriously hurt. They popped their front tires back on, set their handlebars in place, and were off at a much slower pace.

"Can't we catch our breath?" Omar asked Joey.

"Not now," Joey said. "That trick of yours may have saved us from being creeper chow, but it's going to get us noticed, and not by anyone you'd want to meet."

"What were those things?" Omar asked.

"Remember seeing what the Collective did to the people back there?" Joey said, referring to the zombies. "This is what they did to the animals. Or at least the ones they could catch."

They rode on at barely a snail's pace. They put the battlefield behind them and now were entering some foothills.

They rode for another thirty minutes before they heard the helicopters. There were three of them, their spotlights sweeping back and forth across the desert floor. The helicopters were a ways off, back at the battlefield, but it was only a matter of time before they moved on, headed this way, and Joey's crew was still out in the open.

Their route was getting hillier and rockier, which would offer them more protection, but was also slowing them down. A couple of the riders were struggling from wounds they had received earlier, not to mention the pure exhaustion of riding all night.

KRAW!

Omar and Joey heard it at the same time. A hawk's cry. They turned toward an outcropping, and there sat a kestrel, hopping from one foot to another, on a ledge.

The helicopters were dangerously close now.

KRAW!

They headed toward the outcropping, and the kestrel flew off as if its job was done. In the darkness, they spied an area that was blacker than night. A cave. They quickly rode inside and extinguished their flashlights.

"Didn't your grandparents ever tell you to look for scorpions before entering a cave?" A voice cut through the night and silenced their labored breathing.

A familiar voice.

One Omar longed to hear.

"Amy, is that you?" he asked.

8

Whoever it was, didn't bother answering Omar. Instead, she shushed them, and then motioned for them to quickly follow her. They all shouldered their bikes and began their decent into the cave.

They didn't use any lights, not wanting to give the helicopters any sign of their location. All they had to lead them onward was a rope, tied to markers throughout the cave. There were curses as people stubbed toes against rocks and accidently elbowed each other in the pitch black.

About an hour into their hike through the darkness, they saw a glow up ahead. The tunnel opened into a large cavern with lights hanging from the ceiling.

"Welcome to our little hideaway," their guide said, still not turning to face Omar.

Omar looked around, amazed. There was a circle of huts made out of everything from plywood to sheet metal. In the center of the huts was a clearing with a small stage. Off to one side was a cistern, with pipes leading up to the ceiling. And beyond the huts was a garden with lamps hanging down from the ceiling. Several dozen people had gathered to see the newcomers.

"You've expanded since I've last been here, Ames," Joey said.

That's when she turned around, and Omar got his first glance. Like Joey, Amy had aged. The soft round features of her once-youthful face had hardened, and her hair was cropped short. But the feature that stood out most to Omar was the scar running from where her left eye had been all the way back to her left ear.

He was horrified. He wanted to run to her. Hug her. Ask her what had happened. But the grip of Joey's hand on his shoulder told him to be patient.

"Yeah, once we were able to drive holes through the rock above," Amy said in a voice that was deeper than Omar remembered.

"We also hooked up the lights to our solar panels," she added. "We even have some grow lights hooked up to the grind."

"Very impressive," Joey said.

"We were also able to use those same holes to collect dew and rain water," Amy added. "Thus, our new garden."

"And here I've been living off of canned peas and huddling over a fire when you're living the life of luxury," Joey said.

"Joe, I've told you a million times, we should merge our clans and you could live here. We've got the room."

"We can discuss that later. For now, don't you want to talk about our guest here?" Joey looked at Omar.

Amy seemed to be avoiding eye contact with Omar and turned her head away from him to hide the scar.

"Not here," Amy said. Even though she was looking at her feet, Omar could see tears welling up in her eyes. "In my hut. You know where it is."

Joey led Omar away from the crowd while Amy barked out commands to have the newcomers fed and taken care off. "There's also plug-ins if you have any devices that need charging. We even have a music server up and running if you need some new tunes."

***

Inside Amy's hut, Omar flopped onto a chair with a puff of dust. He was exhausted and dirty. Joey poured them each a glass of water from a pitcher that sat on a table in the middle of the room. Then he, too, sat down.

Seconds later, Amy joined them. There was excitement in her step and she looked down at her feet, fidgeting with her hands, as if she were unsure what to do or say. Omar stood and took a step toward her. She leaped into his arms.

"I missed you, O," she cried. "Where did you go?"

"Nowhere," he whispered. "One day, I was back at the base moping because we had just been robbed. The next, I was here."

"You look like you haven't aged a year," Amy said, eyeing him up. She shared that same intense, faraway look that Joey had scanned him with, as if age or near-death experiences had taught them to scrutinize people and situations more closely. "A lot has changed. And not for the better."

Amy poured herself a glass of water and sat down at the table with them.

As Omar listened to his friends catch up, he was amazed by the changes in them.

The youthful softness of their features had been hardened by age and experience. The laughs were quicker, unabashed. Their words were more directed and to the point. Yet, he was sure he still saw a spark of the kids he knew—what he thought was only yesterday—but was now five years later, in their eyes.

"I didn't tell him about Dylan," Joey said, nodding to Omar.

"What about the others. Eldrick, Rafe, and Neelu..." Amy trialed off.

"He knows," Joey said. "But I felt Dylan's story was yours to tell."

Amy looked at her hands, wrapped around her glass of water. "Thanks."

She was crying now, softly. Just enough that her body shook slightly. Then she looked up, struggling to meet Omar's eyes before turning away.

"He's dead, too," her voice cracked.

"I kinda guessed that from Joey's reaction," Omar said softly. "I'm sorry. I know how close you two were."

"It's how he died that hurts," Amy continued. "It happened about a year after the Collective broke into our facility. About a year after you disappeared. I wish you had been there. To lead us."

Amy paused a moment as sobs shook her body. It was odd, to Omar, hearing her wish he had been there to lead them, when from everything he had seen the past few days, proved that Amy and Joey were capable leaders. More so than he had ever been.

Amy continued, "We were out on a mission, trying to get a piece of the Fragment. It was getting harder and harder to locate them, and harder and harder to beat the Collective to the punch. They were winning, and we were desperate.

"As it turns out, we fell into a trap. Rafe and Eldrick had already been killed, so it was just Joey, Neelu, Slider, and me at that point. We were surrounded.

"Your brother, Tommy, was there. He told us that if we gave up our Fragments, he'd let us live. We had already lost you, and after Rafe and Eldrick, I couldn't do it. I couldn't fight anymore. Joey, Neelu, and I decided to give up our Fragments, thinking that at least we'd live to fight another day.

"But Dylan was more stubborn." And Amy's voice began to quaver.

"Yeah, that sounds like Slider," Omar said.

The slight break in the conversation gave Amy a chance to regain her composure.

She continued on after a gulp of water. "Well, he didn't trust Tommy, rightfully so. As soon as we gave up our Fragments, Tommy's goons seized us. But Slider didn't give his up. He fought back. He died helping Joey and I and Neelu escape. Only Neelu didn't escape unharmed. There was nothing we could do!"

Amy broke down crying and collapsed on the table. Omar moved in to comfort her, wrapping his arms around her shoulders.

"I'm so sorry, Omar," Amy cried.

They sat in silence for a long moment, each of them remembering their lost friends, honoring them with their tears.

Slowly at first, they began to talk about their early days in the Revolution. How they met. How awkward and afraid they felt to be part of such a meaningful group. They started sharing old jokes and their tears came more from laughter than sadness.

"This is kinda like old times," Joey said.

"Yeah, I wish it could be like that again," Amy added. "All of us together."

"Why can't it? Why can't it be like old times?" Omar asked. "We can just hunker down here, safe and sound, until we hatch a plan to get the Revolution on its feet."

Amy shot Joey a meaningful glance.

"You didn't tell him, did you?" Amy asked.

Joey looked away and shook his head.

"Tell me what?" Omar asked.

"The zombies," Joey said. "Did you notice that they were all older? No kids."

"I didn't have time to pay that much attention to them," Omar admitted. "I didn't wanna stick around for introductions."

"Well, it's not a disease or anything that made them that way," Amy explained. "It's simply age. The older someone gets, the more likely they'll turn."

"Seriously?" said Omar, shocked.

"I've seen it happen to some of my friends," Amy said. "And we don't know why, or what the Collective did. It just happens."

"When? How old are most people?"

"About twenty," Joey replied.

"And how old are you two?"

"Nineteen," Amy whispered.

Joey didn't answer.

"Joey?" Omar pleaded. "How old are you?"

"You better tell him," Amy said.

"I turned twenty last week."

FRAGMENT
POWER QUES
ENTERED
REVOLUTION VISIO
APOCALYPSE AM
SKATE KESTRE
ENERGY DESTIN

9

Omar had a restless night. He was still unsure of what had happened to him. Why had he been thrown five years into the future. Was it some strange power of his Fragment, or something the Collective had done? Whatever the case, he was now living in a dangerous new world.

He worried about his friends, the few he still had remaining in this world. They were about to be zombified. Omar didn't know how stop it. If there was even anything that could be done.

Was it too late? he wondered.

Then it dawned on Omar. He had something the Collective wanted.

Omar had bargaining power. And a plan hatched.

Slowly, he drifted off to sleep, a devious smile spreading across his face.

***

"No way!" Joey said. "I'm not gonna let you do it."

The next morning, Omar was telling Joey and Amy his plan. They didn't think it was as genius as he had last night.

"It's not that easy, O," Amy agreed. "You can't just waltz into the Collective's compound. Things don't happen that way. People usually get dragged there by zombies."

"We won't be waltzing in. We'll be hitchhiking," Omar explained.

"Okay, O," Joey said. "Let's say you can hijack one of their helicopters. What then? What next?"

Omar leaned forward. "You ever go into a competition as an underdog?" he began. "You know, back when we used to skate and bike and snowboard for fun? Remember how the favorites would sometimes get a little cocky. Be a little too confident. That often leads to sloppy skating, when you think you don't have to try as hard. You forget the golden rule, 'go big, or go home.'

"That's when the underdog catches you off guard. He's trying harder than you to hit his tricks, and is pushing things to the limits of his ability, like Tony Hawk did when he completed the first 900. Did you know it took him more than a dozen tries at the X Games before he actually completed that trick?

"Granted, he wasn't an underdog. But we are. And I'm guessing that the Collective is now overly confident and getting sloppy. They won't be expecting us to hit their compound."

"So your plan," Amy said, "is pretty much to get in, get whatever Fragment they have at the nearest compound, and then get out."

"Yeah."

"Better than sitting around worried waiting to become zombified," Amy said. "You in, Joe?"

"Like I have a choice?" Joey said.

***

They took the rest of the day to prepare. Then, with six other kids—three from Clan Rail and three from Clan Kestrel—they formed three teams and headed out. They crossed the desert on BMX bikes, wanting to put a few hours distance between them and Clan Kestrel's hangout.

Atop a large sand dune, they stopped and dismounted.

"It's all up to you, O," Joey said.

Omar pulled his Fragment from his front pants pocket. Clutching it in both hands, he raised it skyward. Blue energy crackled around his fists as he scrunched up his face in concentration. Then a blue bolt erupted, lighting up the sky.

"So now we wait," Amy said.

"Yeah," Omar replied. He felt a little lightheaded from all the energy that had just coursed through him.

Joey set his pack down and pulled out a can of peas. "Might as well eat while we're at it."

They didn't have to wait long. Within twenty minutes, three Black Hawk helicopters roared over a distant sand dune and headed straight for them.

Two of the helicopters hovered overhead, fifty feet off the ground with guns trained on them. The third landed at the foot of the dune.

Two men and one woman, dressed in black from head to toe, leaped out of the chopper. They trudged their way up the dune to confront Joey, Amy, and Omar.

"You have the missing Fragment," the tallest of the trio said. "Give it to me, and we'll let you live."

"You'll let us live, huh?" Omar said with a sneer. "I have the Fragment."

Omar extended his hand outward to the man, not to hand the Fragment to him, but to show the wheel to the trio. The Collective agent's eyes were filled with both awe and fear, seeing how it crackled with life in Omar's hand.

"And you think you have the upper hand." Omar laughed.

Omar held up his fist and pointed it at one of the hovering helicopters. A blue bolt of energy shot from his hand and struck the helicopter. It was sent spinning and swirling, out of control.

The three Collective soldiers leaped toward Omar, but Joey and Amy blocked their way.

Then Omar struck the second helicopter, and it started spinning out of control.

Both of them crashed in an explosion of metal and flame. Collective soldiers crawled out of the wreckage, and the members of Joey's and Amy's clans were there to disarm them.

Omar aimed his fist at the remaining helicopter.

"Now, it's my turn to make the demands," Omar said. He was amazed by the confident tone in his voice.

It was as if he had been learning a thing or two about leadership and taking charge from the older versions of his friends.

The three Collective agents looked down at their feet, defeated.

"First, we're going to borrow your helicopter and pilot," Omar said. "Well, first we're actually going to borrow your uniforms, so start undressing."

***

They were still feeling elated as the helicopter approached the Collective's compound. It lay at the edge of Phoenix. It looked like the Collective had taken over one of the larger mansions in town. The house was a huge stucco affair, with several other buildings and a swimming pool that had been drained. A high fence surrounded the compound, and pressed against the barrier were row upon row of zombies.

When the helicopter landed, Omar saw a figure from his past step from the mansion and storm toward the helicopter and it wasn't a sight for sore eyes. Rather it was an old nemesis, Twitch. He was screaming and gusts from the helicopters rotor blades tossed his thick black hair about.

"Where are the other two copters?" Twitch yelled at the top of his lungs.

Joey, then Amy, and lastly Omar stepped out of the helicopter. They were dressed in Collective black, but that didn't seem to fool Twitch. He stopped dead in his tracks as their sight. The uniforms hung oddly on the trio and didn't fool Twitch for a second.

"Oh crap!" he said, quickly turning to the mansion's back doors.

The Kestrel and Rail clan members quickly leaped from the helicopter. They couldn't bring their BMX bikes, but they were armed with the handlebar clubs and wheel shields.

They quickly spread out to scout the area for any bad guys, while Omar chased down Twitch.

He caught up with him at the edge of an empty swimming pool.

"The Collective thought you were dead, man," Twitch said. "But I always knew you'd come back. And when I sensed a Fragment near...even though my superiors said it had to be the other missing piece, I knew it was you."

"The *other* Fragment?" Omar asked.

"Yeah, there's two missing artifacts," said Twitch. "We thought one was buried with you, but we have no idea where the other one is.

"We haven't felt its presence for years," added Twitch, "and we've scoured the planet inside and out."

"So why haven't you been zombified like the rest of them," Omar said, turning his gaze to the perimeter fence. He was trying to distract Twitch while Joey and Amy snuck around him. But as they were talking, Twitch dug into his pants pocket and pulled out a sliver of deck, his own Fragment.

"This," Twitch said. Red energy engulfed his fist. "Now you two keep back," he said to Amy and Joey, who were just meters away from him on either side.

Just then, the fence collapsed around the compound, and the zombies rushed forward. Joey, Omar, Amy, and the members of their clan quickly gathered by the side of the empty pool. They were surrounded and blocked from helicopter by screaming bodies.

Omar pulled out his Fragment, held it high, and shot a blue bolt into the sky.

The zombies stopped. What remained of the Revolution stood in a semicircle, clubs drawn, with Omar standing in their middle.

"I figured it was you," Twitch said. "I sensed a piece of the Fragment was near and knew you wouldn't be as easy to fool as those two were."

Twitch looked over at Joey and Amy. "So I set up this elaborate trap," he said. "I control the local zombies with this."

Twitch raised his hand, and the red eyes of the zombies pulsed in rhythm with the red electricity that engulfed Twitch's hand.

"I also know that you won't give up that Fragment if I ask nicely," Twitch said.

"You're right," Omar replied.

"So here's the deal. I let your friends go—"

"Just like you let Dylan go!" Amy screamed at him. "Just like you let Neelu go!"

"Ames." Joey tried soothing her.

Twitch raised his hands, and the zombies parted like the Red Sea, forming a path that lead to the helicopter.

"And what to you want from me?" Omar asked.

"A little competition," Twitch said. "See, I've emptied out this swimming pool. The Bowl, I call it. It's where I invite all my friends to come play with me." An evil grin lit up Twitch's face. "You willin' to go old school?"

"You know he's not going to let you go," Amy whispered into Omar's ear.

"I know," replied Omar. "That's why I need to beat him at his own game."

"And if you do, what then? You're surrounded by thousands of zombies," Joey said.

"Joey, this was my plan. I got us into this. So let me follow it through," Omar said. "I beat him five years ago. I can out-skate him now."

Amy grabbed Omar's free hand in hers. "When you do," she said, looking down at her wrist. "There is a way out."

Omar's eyes followed hers, and what he saw stunned him. A hawk tattoo, the decal from Tony Hawk's 900 board, transferred from Amy's hands to his, and then slid up his arm, out of sight. He felt a tingle against his skin.

"You—" Omar begin.

"We have to go," Amy interrupted him. "Come on, Joey."

Omar watched the members of Clan Rail and Clan Kestrel load into the helicopter. As it lifted off the ground, Joey and Amy hung out its open side door, gazing down at him. There was a sadness in their eyes. Omar was hoping that this wasn't the last time. Then he turned back to Twitch.

"Okay, if we're going to do this," Omar said, "let me get out of these Collective rags."

OMAR VERSUS TWITCH

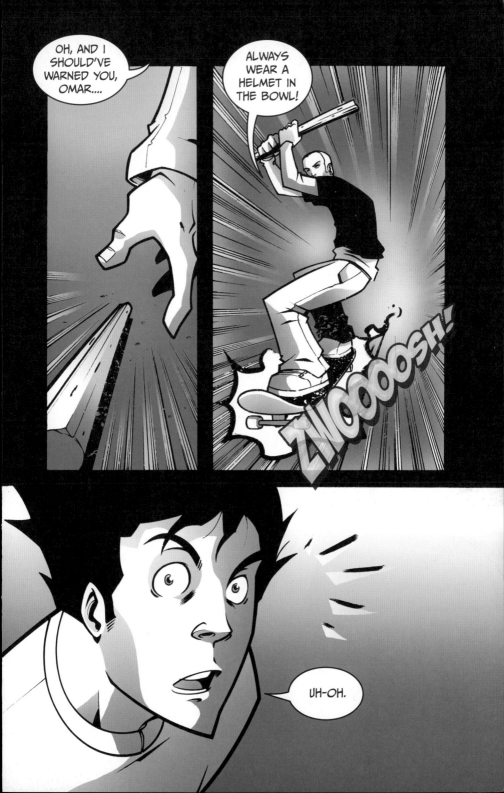

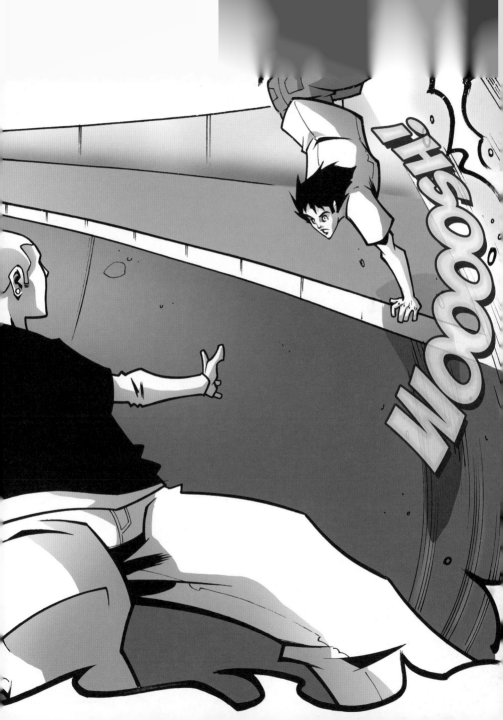

10

Omar felt energy coursing through his whole body. He had never used the hawk decal Fragment to transform into a hawk, and it both frightened and amazed him. He was stunned as his arms shrank and feathers sprouted from his hair follicles. His skate shoes disappeared from his feet. They retracted and began to twist into talons.

KRAW! He screamed. And the zombies' hands that had lifted him off of Twitch fell away. They were as shocked and amazed as he was.

As a hawk, Omar hovered in midair for a brief moment once he had been released. Then some deep instinct took over.

Omar spread his wings and, in one swoop, he was above the heads of the zombies. With another flap of his wings, he was beyond the reach of their outstretched hands. The next, he was above the roof of the mansion.

"Get down here!" Twitch yelled.

Then a baseball bat flew past.

Another couple swoops of his wings, and the zombies below had shrunk to the size of ants. Nothing could reach him now.

Off in the distance, he saw the helicopter that carried Joey and Amy away. He was surprised that his sight allowed him to see it that far away.

He thought about flying after it, but something else caught his attention. In the distance, a small black speck flew low along the horizon. He felt an emptiness in his stomach as he gave chase.

The bird wasn't very fast, and Omar caught up with it in no time. But when he did, he didn't dive down to attack, even though a nagging urge wanted him to. What held him back was that the bird was a grebe, a waterfowl. A bird that shouldn't be here in the desert. A bird that was his namesake, Omar Grebes.

He flew above the bird, following its path.

KRAW! He called down to it.

The grebe turned to look up at Omar, and he expected it to freak out in fear, but instead the grebe turned to face him in midair. They, the grebe and the hawk, hovered a hundred meters above the ground, flapping their wings and just staring at each other.

Then the grebe opened its beak, "Omar."

Omar nearly flipped out. Not only did the grebe speak his name, but it did so in a voice that he could never forget. A voice he thought had been swallowed by the waves back in sunny California. A voice that sounded all too much like Zeke Grebes.

"Dad?" Omar asked hesitantly.

The grebe swooped downed and landed on a telephone pole. Omar followed, landing next to the smaller bird.

"I've missed you, son," the grebe said.

Omar couldn't believe what was happening. It seemed like some whacked-out trip from a strange dreamland.

"Is that really you, Dad?" Omar asked. "I mean, are you really alive?"

"I am," his dad replied. "But I'm in hiding."

"Why? Why are you hiding from me? I missed you."

And if hawks could cry, tears would be streaming down Omar's beak.

"I can't tell you now. Let's just say there are secrets about the Revolution that you don't know yet."

"How do I find you again?" asked Omar.

"Seek out Wyvern."

"Who?" questioned Omar.

"Wyvern," the grebe repeated. "Half snake and half bird. She will help you."

The wind whipped up and ruffled their feathers.

"She's the link between the Revolution and the Collective. She's the one that will lead you to me."

Just then, Omar heard a shotgun blast. Feathers flew everywhere as pellets ripped them from the grebes' body. Then the bird began to wobble weakly on its claws.

"Omar..." the grebe called.

"Omar..." The bird fell from its perch.

"Omar..."

There was another blast. Omar felt stabs of fire enter his body. The air around him was filled with feathers and blood.

"*Omar...*" He heard a voice calling. Not his dad's, this time, but one very familiar.

"Omar..." It was a girl's voice.

Neelu's.

"Come on, Omar, wake up!"

11

Omar felt a pillow smother his face.

Panicked, he reached up, grabbing two thin wrists, and pulled.

"Hey," Neelu shouted.

As Omar tugged at her wrists, Neelu was lifted off her feet, and tumbled into bed next to Omar.

"You're alive!" he shouted.

"Yeah, duh," she said. "Though, I wasn't sure you were."

"So what, trying to finish me off?" said Omar.

"Just checking to see if you were playing dead or not," Neelu replied.

Then they were silent for a moment as they looked into each other's eyes. Omar didn't think he had kissed Neelu since their first encounter. And actually, that was just her giving him a quick peck on the cheek.

He leaned over to her and pressed his lips against hers. They were soft and warm, and he was pleasantly surprised to feel them pressing back against his.

"Neelu?" They heard Eldrick call from outside Omar's room. "Did you find Omar?"

Quickly Neelu and Omar broke apart.

Eldrick poked his head around the corner, seeing his daughter and Omar. A funny looked crossed his face, one of approval, as if he could tell that the two teens had just shared a private moment, and that he accepted it. That he was okay with him and Neelu possibly dating.

"Well, come on, you two," Eldrick said. "These boxes aren't going to pack themselves." And he tossed two boxes playfully at the pair.

"What's going on?" Omar said, turning to Neelu.

"We're ditching this place," Neelu said. "The Collective knows about it, so we're moving out."

"Dylan, Amy, and Joey are almost all packed," said Eldrick. "We're just waiting on you two."

Seeing Neelu and Eldrick that they were alive, and then hearing Dylan's name, that he too was alive, all the puzzle pieces came together. Omar understood what he had been through. He had just had a vision. The most real and intense vision yet.

Suddenly, he jumped out of bed, ignoring the pain in his knee. The raspberries coloring his arm. The sting of the coping shaped welt across his back. He slipped on a T-shirt and khakis, stuffed his feet into his skate shoes, and headed out the door.

"Hey, where you going?" Neelu called after him.

Omar ran down the hall. He heard his friends laughing in the kitchen. Joey was telling jokes trying to get Dylan to snort orange juice out his nose, and Amy was berating them.

Omar burst in on them, out of breath.

"Hey, O," Amy said.

"What's up?' Joey said.

"Dude, you look like you've seen a ghost," Dylan added as Omar stared at him in happy disbelief.

Omar shouted, "Guys, you're not going to believe the vision I had last night."

ABOUT TONY HAWK

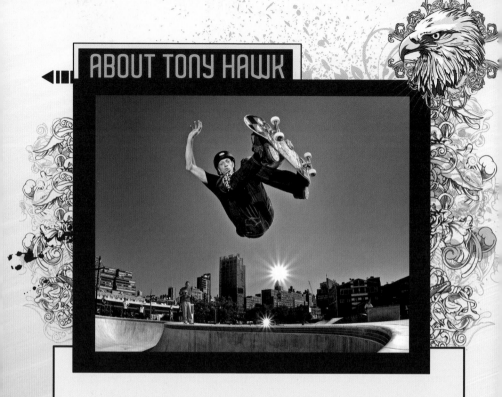

TONY HAWK is the most famous and influential skateboarder of all time. In the 1980s and 1990s, he was instrumental in skateboarding's transformation from fringe pursuit to respected sport. After retiring from competitions in 2000, Tony continues to skate demos and tour all over the world.

He is the founder, President, and CEO of Tony Hawk Inc., which he continues to develop and grow. He is also the founder of the Tony Hawk Foundation, which works to create skateparks and empower youth in low income communities.

ABOUT THE AUTHOR_

BLAKE A. HOENA grew up in central Wisconsin, where, in his youth, he wrote stories about robots conquering the Moon and trolls lumbering around in the woods behind his parents house. Later, he moved to Minnesota to pursue a Masters of Fine Arts degree in Creative Writing from Minnesota State University, Mankato. Since graduating, Blake has written more than forty books for children.

AUTHOR Q & A_

Q: DO YOU PARTICIPATE IN ACTION SPORTS? HOW HAVE THEY INFLUENCED YOU?

A: I like to hit trails with my mountain bike. After a hard, sweaty ride, I feel pretty relaxed and clear-headed. Then I can sit at my computer to crank out a few hundred words.

Q: DESCRIBE YOUR APPROACH TO THE TONY HAWK'S 900 REVOLUTION SERIES.

A: I haven't been on a skateboard since before Tony Hawk did his celebrated 900, so I started off by watching A LOT of YouTube videos of different tricks to get some ideas.

Q: ANY FUTURE PLANS FOR THE TONY HAWK'S 900 REVOLUTION SERIES?

A: Yeah, I'm hoping to write another volume in the series. These characters are a lot of fun, and I don't want the story to end.

OMAR GREBES_
CODE NAME: STALEFISH

AGE: 15

HOMETOWN: Imperial Beach, California

SPORT: Skateboarding

INTERESTS: Punk, Food, and Girls

BIO: An active fifteen-year-old boy, Omar Grebes never slows down. When he's not shredding concrete at Ocean Beach Skatepark, he's kicking through surf at Imperial Beach or scarfing down fish tacos from the nearest roadside shop. His wiry, six-foot frame can't hide his live-or-die lifestyle—scars on his elbows, fresh road rash on his knees, and a first-degree sunburn on his nose. However, Omar's not afraid to show off these "battle scars"—often wearing little more than a T-shirt, board shorts, and a pair of black skate shoes. The Bones Brigade and the SoCal surf culture have heavily influenced his personal and skating style. At the park or on the street, Omar is as clean, creative, and inventive as they come.

DYLAN CROW_
CODE NAME: SLIDER

AGE: 14

HOMETOWN: New York City

SPORT: Skateboarding

INTERESTS: Hip-hop, the Yankees, gaming

BIO: When you skate in New York, it's all about getting creative, and fourteen-year-old Dylan Crow considers himself a street artist. You won't catch him tagging the alley walls like some of his friends; instead he paints the streets with his board. This stylish teen rarely hits the skate parks. He wants to be seen grinding rails in Brooklyn, doing ollies in Central Park, and launching kickflips in Midtown. He's heavily influenced by some of today's top young skaters, including Ryan Sheckler, Chris Cole, and Paul Rodriguez. His smooth skating style matches his personal appearance, which is born in hip-hop and indie-rock music—cocked Yankees cap, graphic T-shirt, clean khakis, and custom kicks.

AMY KESTREL_
CODE NAME: BANSHEE

AGE: 14

HOMETOWN: Telluride, Colorado

SPORT: Snowboarding

INTERESTS: Clothes, Gear, and Travel

BIO: Fourteen-year-old Amy Kestrel is a powder pig. Often hidden beneath five layers of hoodies, this bleached blond CO ski bum is tough to spot on the street. However, get her on the slopes, and she's hard to miss. Shredding since the age of three, Amy's well-to-do parents support her ambitions both emotionally and financially. She's always got the latest and greatest gear—custom boards, top-of-the-line boots, and killer shades. Unfortunately, Amy lacks one thing—confidence. At Breck, Telli, or A-Basin, you'll often find her hiding in the pow-pow instead of showing off in the terrain park. But get her alone on the slopes, and she'll prove that posh apparel doesn't make the boarder. It's all about going big and going bold, much like her idols Kelly Clark and Shaun White.

JOEY RAIL_
CODE NAME: RAIL

AGE: 14

HOMETOWN: Moab, Utah

SPORT: BMX Freestyle

INTERESTS: Animal Rights, Environmental Activism, Outdoors

BIO: Growing up in Moab, fourteen-year-old Joey Rail learned to ride before he could walk. He's tried every two-wheeled sport imaginable (motocross, mountain biking, etc.), but he's always come back to BMX freestyle. The skill, patience, and power required for this daring sport suit his personality. Joey is an outdoor enthusiast and loves taking things to the edge. On days that he's not competing, he's skinning his knees on the red stone of Slickrock Trail, cliff jumping off the banks of Lake Powell, or rafting down the Red River. You'll never find him wearing anything other than jeans and a T-shirt—except, of course, on a moonlit training ride. On those nights, he'll throw on a dusty flannel to protect again the cool desert winds.

STORY SETTING: Desert

TONY HAWK'S 900 revolution

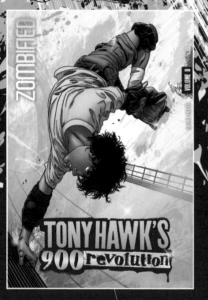

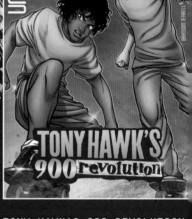

TONY HAWK'S 900 REVOLUTION, VOL. 9: ZOMBIFIED

Once more beset by visions, Omar finds himself trapped inside one. The world he sees is vastly different than the one he left. In this postapocalyptic vision, the Collective has defeated the Revolution. In their absence, the disbanded Revolution has been replaced by a group of tribes that skate in their honor. Omar searches for his friends, for the meaning behind this horrific vision, and for a way out!

TONY HAWK'S 900 REVOLUTION, VOL. 10: UNEARTHED

Omar convinces Eldrick Otus to him lead the Revolution on a t to recover a Fragment in Egy When they discover the Fragme is resting deep within a forgott pyramid, Omar sends Joey a Amy after it. The Collective, led Elliot Addison, causes the pyramid entrance to collapse. The tee must work together to retrieve t Fragment and find a way out befo

QUEST CONTINUES...

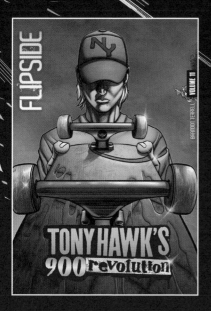

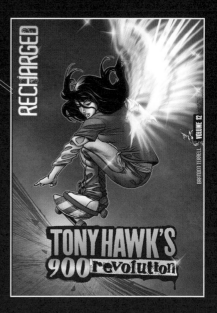

TONY HAWK'S 900 REVOLUTION, VOL. 11: FLIPSIDE

The Collective, in possession of the Fragmented board and growing stronger every day, decides to retrieve one of their own: Tommy Goff, held captive by the Revolution in an undisclosed location. To discover the prisoner's whereabouts, Elliot Addison and his mentor Archard Venin must earn the Revolution's trust. But Archard has other plans — the destruction of the Revolution, and the death of his old friend, Eldrick Otus.

TONY HAWK'S 900 REVOLUTION, VOL. 12: RECHARGED

Omar Grebes and the team meet Fiona Skylark. Shrapnel from a childhood accident is embedded in the girl's stomach. One of the pieces is from the 900 board, making Fiona a walking, talking Fragment. The team must keep her safe from the Collective. The biggest shock is yet to come, though, when Omar comes face to face with a very much alive Zeke Grebes, who invites them to join 'The New Revolution!

UNEARTHED

"Oh man, I am so out of my league."

There weren't too many things that frazzled Dylan
Crow. In fact, he'd earned the nickname Slider because
of his knack for finding a way out of any sticky
situation. And lately there'd been many. As a member
of the 900 Revolution, a super-secret team of teens
who were searching for Fragments of Tony Hawk's
fabled 900 skateboard, Slider had faced numerous near-
death run-ins with a group of evil baddies known as
The Collective. He'd been framed in a blackmail plot
that had branded him a traitor and left him temporarily
exiled from the Revolution. And he'd helped the team
relocate from Phoenix—where the Fragments of the
mystical skateboard had been stolen—to Seattle.

Through it all, Slider had found a way to let
everything, well, slide, off him. "Like water off a duck's
back," his foster brother Mikey would have said with
that goofy grin of his.

Having faced all this and more, Slider never thought
he'd be completely baffled by something as ridiculous as
a restaurant menu.

He held the red velvet menu in front of him, trying to read the dinner specials and failing miserably.

"I can't even pronounce half of these words," he grumbled.

"Yeah," came a voice from the other side of the menu. "It's all in French."

Slider peered over his menu and across the table at a smiling Amy Kestrel. Amy was a fellow Revolution member and Slider's new girlfriend. Kind of. Sort of. He thought. They hadn't actually used the words boyfriend and girlfriend yet. In fact, they hadn't even kissed, except the one time in New York, when Slider had saved Amy's rather nice-looking bacon from the Collective. There was something about constantly trying to save the world that made such formalities hard to sort out. He dug her, though. That was pretty easy to understand.

Amy tucked a strand of blonde hair behind her ear and whispered, "Don't worry. I can't read them either."

The two of them were dining in the swankiest restaurants Slider had ever seen. Around them, other couples sat at candlelit tables devouring fresh seafood. At fourteen years old, Slider and Amy were the youngest people in the restaurant by two decades.

Slider looked uncomfortably at the table next to them, where a heaping plate of food, topped with a fish whose head was still firmly attached to its cooked body, was being delivered.

"How did you hear about this place?" Amy asked.

Slider shrugged. "Online."

"And why exactly did you want to come here?"

"It got rave reviews," said Slider. "Like five-star reviews. That's good, right?"

Amy laughed. "Sure," she replied. "But why did you think we'd enjoy it?"

"Well," Slider quietly responded, "it's our first date. I wanted it to be special." The sentiment lingered.

"Dylan, I already know it's special," Amy confessed.

"You do?" Slider asked.

"Yeah, because you're not wearing your Yankees hat," she said with a smirk.

Slider smoothed out his shaggy hair. He was trying to look his best, but he felt naked without his lucky cap.

Poring over the menu's looping script, Slider said, "I'm going to go out on a limb and guess that *Petoncles Ail Bouillabaisse* doesn't translate to cheeseburger."

"That's a shame," Amy said. "I love cheeseburgers."

"You wanna cut out?" asked Slider.

"I would love to, Dylan."

"Then let's get out of here," he said, "Before I accidentally order something with eyes."

Amy laughed and grabbed his hand. Together, they out of the restaurant and into the cool Seattle night.

Slider snatched a pair of skateboards from behind a large potted plant outside the restaurant, where he and Amy had squirreled them away earlier. They rattled down the sidewalk, into the heart of the city.

Amy, a gifted snowboarder who'd spent her whole life carving powder, was also adept on a skateboard. She looked comfortable, poised, and alert.

Slider had fallen for Amy the first time he saw her in Colorado, when she was recruited into the Revolution. Every time she was around, his stomach felt like he'd just dropped off the coping of a halfpipe.

With the skyline—and the iconic Space Needle—as a backdrop, Slider watched Amy ollie high into the air and perform a textbook backside 50/50 grind on a bike rack. The metal sang beneath her board as the truck hangers locked on the rack. It was a beautiful sound that Slider never tired of hearing. He could see the blue glow of Amy's Fragment from her pocket as it enhanced her already extreme talent. Amy dismounted off the rail, landing beside him.

"Not too shabby, Ames" he said, acting unimpressed.

"Let's see what you've got, Slider," she responded, emphasizing his nickname. She was the only person who refused to call him by anything other than Dylan.

"Watch and learn!" Slider spied a long set of cement steps winding down to a plaza. The crackle of blue electricity from his Fragment pulse through his feet, up his legs, and into his heart.

He danced on the board and switched to ride fakie. Then he kickflipped up and balanced the deck on the rail in a backward boardslide. Attempting to make the advanced trick appear effortless, he blew Amy a kiss as he left her at the top of the steps. The board slid down the rail. At the bottom, he heelflipped off the rail and back onto solid ground.

Amy whistled and applauded.

"Thank you!" Slider said with a bow.

The duo rode their boards to the diner Amy had seen earlier. They ordered burgers and fries and sat at one of the diner's outdoor tables. Then they casually boarded through the city, talking about everything. Slider's experiences growing up in foster care in New York. What it was like for Amy to have an FBI agent for a father. The only topic off-limits was Mikey, Slider's foster brother who had suspiciously disappeared.

Through it all, Slider couldn't shake the notion that they were being watched. As they rode along a sidewalk, Slider looked back along the street. There, idling alongside the curb, was a familiar black HumVee.

"Is that Rafe?" Slider asked.

Amy followed his gaze. Then she nodded. "Yeah."

"Unbelievable." Slider waved at the vehicle. "Hey, Captain Buzzkill! Hope you're having a great evening!" His wave morphed into a one-fingered salute.

"Dylan!" Amy grabbed his waggling hand.

"What?" asked Slider. "We both know he's following us because he doesn't trust me. None of them do."

It was true. Slider's role in the Revolution was still on shaky ground following the incident in Mexico.

The Collective had blown up an ancient temple and had nearly taken out the Revolution team with it. Warren Rafe, the teens' no-nonsense mentor, had later found incriminating evidence the Collective had planted in Slider's pack. He had forced the teen into exile.

Since Slider's return, the reception he'd received from Rafe had been downright frigid.

Read more in the next adventure of . . .

Tony Hawk's 900 Revolution

TONY HAWK'S
900 revolution